E
MCC

McClure, Gillian

Prickly pig

Cop 1

PRICKLY PIG

Gillian McClure

ANDRE DEUTSCH

First published September 1976 by André Deutsch Limited
105 Great Russell Street London WC1
Second impression May 1979

Reproduction by Paramount Litho Company Wickford Essex
Filmset by Keyspools Ltd Golborne Lancashire
Printed in Singapore by Tien Wah Press (Pte) Limited,

ISBN 0 233 96780 X

First published in the United States of America 1980

Library of Congress Number 79 51014

OLYMPIC HILLS

The wind blew and shook the trees.
A falling leaf flicked
the hedgehog's snout.
"If the leaves are falling,
winter must be close.
I'll have to look out for a home
and take my long sleep,"
he thought.

The hedgehog came upon a fence
and squeezed himself under it.
He saw a farm hen's nest with eggs inside.
The hedgehog began to sniff.
"A fine warm nest with delicious eggs.
This will make a winter home."

But the farm hen came back . . .
She clucked and squawked, she fussed and flapped.
"Get out of my nest you prickly pig.
You're no egg, you hard-boiled villain.
I shall peck you, peck, peck at your nose
until every prickle of you goes!"
"What a flap these hens work themselves into.
I couldn't share her nest all winter,
she wouldn't let me get one wink of sleep."
And the hedgehog hurried away.

The wind blew cold
and shook the trees.
Two leaves fell
on to the hedgehog's snout.
He snuffed the air and thought:
"Prickles won't keep me warm.
I need a place
away from the wind."

The hedgehog found
a barn and crept into
the cow stall.
"I will make this
my winter home,
if the cow would just
move up an inch
and spare me
some milk too."

"Moo, move!
You're pricking me, pig, and stealing my milk.
I'll toss you up and over my head.
I'll have no hedgehog in *my* bed."
The hedgehog tumbled onto his back.
"Bad tempered old cow.
She'll turn her milk sour,"
he grunted and hurried away.

The hedgehog shuffled through a hedge.

He came to a rabbit burrow
and peered in.

"I'll try down here," he thought.

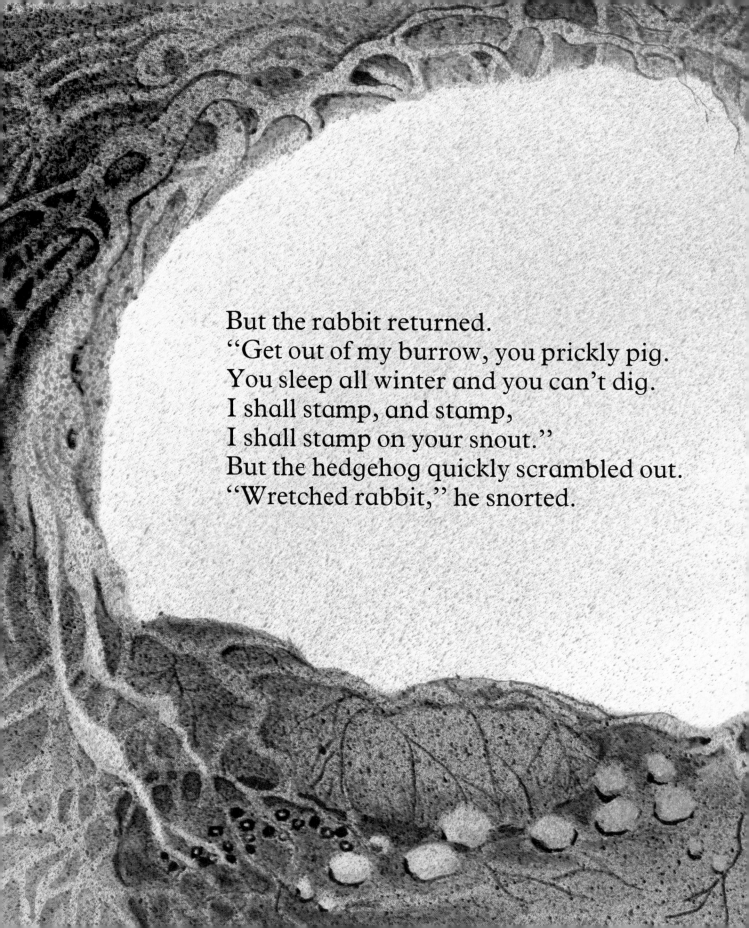

But the rabbit returned.
"Get out of my burrow, you prickly pig.
You sleep all winter and you can't dig.
I shall stamp, and stamp,
I shall stamp on your snout."
But the hedgehog quickly scrambled out.
"Wretched rabbit," he snorted.

The wind blew and shook the trees.
More leaves fell
on to the hedgehog's snout.
He yawned and crept into
a dark wood where mists brewed
and foxes lurked.

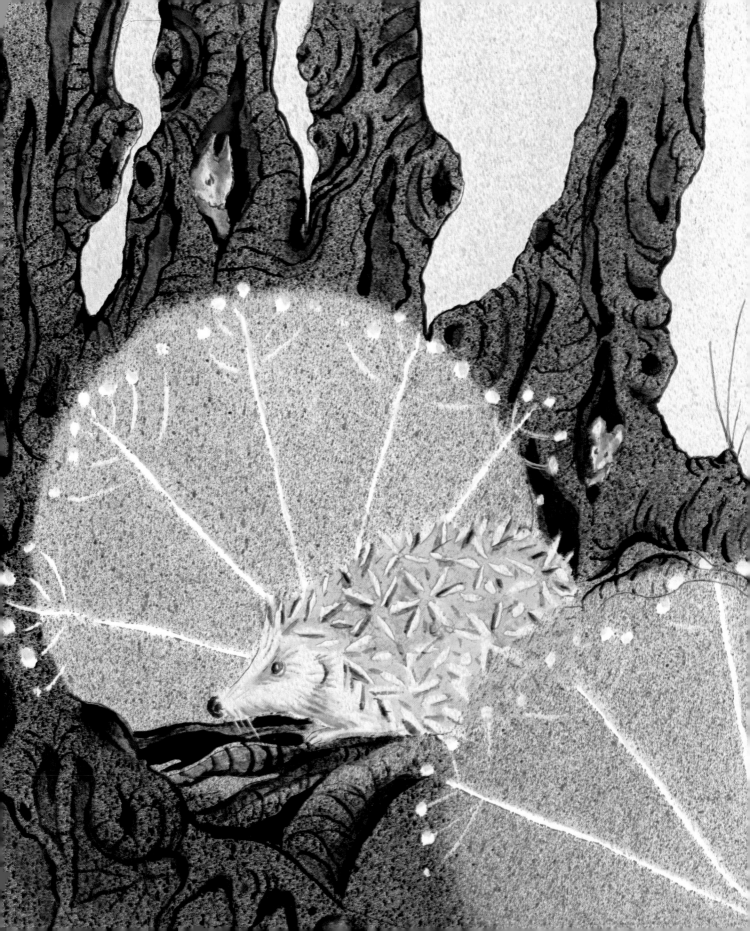

A fox with greedy eyes
came out of the shadows.
"Why, a juicy pig
beneath those prickles.
Come and live in my house.
We can eat dinner together."
"Oh no, no. I know your kind.
I'll be *in* you when you have dined."
And the hedgehog rolled up
into a tight ball of prickles.
"Then I'll play with this
prickly ball," barked the fox.
"I'll roll my dinner down the hill."

OLYMPIC HILLS

Through one eye open,
the hedgehog saw the sky
roll over the ground and the ground
roll over the sky.

Splash! The ground
had become water all around.
The hedgehog swam to a bank
and dragged himself
out of the water.

The wind blew and shook the trees.
Leaves were falling fast.
They stuck to his prickles. The
hedgehog shivered and closed one eye.
The leaves fell faster. They began
to cover up the hedgehog's prickles.
He closed the other eye.

The wind blew and shook the trees.
No leaves fell, for the trees were bare
and winter had come.
But where was the hedgehog?